The Fir Tree

The Fir Tree

Based on the Fairy Tale by
HANS CHRISTIAN ANDERSEN

illustrated by
DIANE GOODE

Random House · New York

Out in the forest stood a pretty little fir tree. It had plenty of sunlight and fresh air, and all around grew many larger trees of all kinds. But the little fir tree was not happy. It took no pleasure in the sunshine and fresh air. It took no notice of the peasant children who came to look for strawberries. They would sit by the little fir tree and say, "How pretty and small this tree is!" The fir tree did not like to hear that at all! It only wanted to be great and big.

When it was winter and the snow lay sparkling all around, a hare would often come along and jump right over the little fir tree. This made the fir tree so angry!

"Rejoice in your youth," said the sunbeams. "Rejoice in your fresh growth and young life!"

But the fir tree did not understand. "Oh, if only I were as big as the others!" it said with a sigh. "Then I would spread my branches far around, and birds would build nests in my boughs, and I would nod grandly in the wind!"

Two winters went by, and when the third came, the tree had grown so tall that the hare had to run around it.

"Oh! To grow and grow and become old—it's the finest thing in the world!" the tree thought happily.

When Christmas time was near, many young trees were cut down and taken away on wagons. But not the fir tree.

"Where are they all going?" asked the fir tree. "Where are they being taken?"

"We know!" chirped the sparrows. "We looked in the town windows. We know where they go!"

"They are put into warm rooms and dressed up in the most beautiful splendor," said the sparrows. "Gilt apples, honey cakes, toys, and hundreds of candles. They are called Christmas trees."

"Oh! How I long to be a Christmas tree!" cried the fir tree. "It is my greatest wish."

All year long the fir tree grew, and when Christmas came again, its wish came true. It was the first tree to be cut down. The axe cut deep, and the tree fell to the ground with a great sigh.

"I thought I would feel happy to leave," thought the tree. "But it is sad to leave my friends and my home."

The fir tree was no sooner taken to a yard when a man came and said, "This tree is perfect!"

So the fir tree was taken to a large house and put into a tub filled with sand. Then the servants and young ladies hung golden apples and walnuts from the branches. Dolls and toy soldiers swung on satin ribbons, and more than a hundred colored candles were fastened to different boughs. On the top was fixed a glittering gold star.

"This evening," said the young ladies, "this tree will shine and shine!"

The tree could hardly wait for evening to come!

At last evening came, and the candles were lighted. What a brilliant sight!

"I wonder if the sparrows will come and admire me!" thought the tree. "Will I grow here and be dressed so beautifully all year long? How wonderful that would be!"

Suddenly the parlor doors were thrown open, and the children rushed in. They danced gleefully around the tree, and one present after another was plucked from it. The children rushed about so forcefully that branches cracked and the tree nearly fell down.

"What next?" the fir tree wondered, feeling confused and a little sad.

"Tell us a story!" shouted the children as they drew a little fat man toward the tree. He sat down beneath it and told the story of Klumpey-Dumpey, who had great troubles, yet married the princess and lived happily ever after. The children clapped their hands. The fir tree had never heard such a wonderful story before.

"Surely I will live happily ever after too," it thought. "I will be dressed every evening with candles and toys, nuts and fruit. How jealous the trees in the forest would be if they could see me then!"

The fir tree stood quiet and thoughtful all night, thinking of its bright future.

In the morning the servants came into the parlor.

"Now I will be dressed again!" thought the foolish tree.

But the servants dragged the tree upstairs to the attic and threw it in a dark corner.

"What am I to do here?" thought the tree. "What will happen to me now?"

Days and nights went by and nobody came to the attic. "Perhaps they want to shelter me from the snow until spring comes," the fir tree said. "If only it were not so dark and lonely here—there isn't even a little hare to visit me!"

"Squeak, squeak!" said two little mice as they crept toward the tree. "Hello, old Christmas tree!"

"I'm not old," said the tree indignantly.

"Tell us where you come from," said the mice. They were very curious. "Tell us about the most beautiful spot on earth! Have you been there?"

"I don't know," replied the tree. "But I know the forest, where the sun shines and the birds sing." And the tree told them all about its youth.

"Oh, how happy you must have been!" said the mice.

"Happy?" said the tree thoughtfully. "Yes—I suppose I was quite happy."

The next night the mice came with four other mice. "Tell us another story!" they said.

So the fir tree told of when it had been hung with golden fruit and toys and lighted candles.

"How merry you must have been!" cried the mice. "What a splendid story!"

The next night a great many mice appeared, and even two rats. The fir tree told them the story of Klumpey-Dumpey, who married the princess.

"Tell us another!" said the rats.

"I don't know any other stories," said the fir tree. So the mice and rats left the attic, and the fir tree was alone once again.

"It was nice when the curious little mice listened to me," sighed the fir tree. "But now that, too, is past. I will be so happy when they take me out of this attic!"

At last one morning people came and dragged the old fir tree outside into the garden. Tulips waved in the breeze, and all the trees were covered with pink blossoms.

"Now I shall live!" said the tree, and it tried to spread its branches proudly. But they were all brittle and yellow. The tree lay forlornly in a corner among the weeds. A boy came and tore the gold star from it. Then he jumped on the branches till they broke.

The fir tree looked at the lovely garden and then at itself. It thought of its youth in the forest and of Christmas Eve and of the little mice in the attic.

"I was happy and I never even knew it!" said the old tree. "I always wanted something else. Now it's all past— gone forever!"

Then the servant came and set fire to the tree. It blazed brightly and sighed deeply, thinking of its happy past and how foolish it had been. Each sigh was like a little shot. And then the tree was burned to ashes.

A Little Library
of Christmas Classics

With illustrations
by Diane Goode

Christmas Carols

The Fir Tree
Based on the Fairy Tale
by Hans Christian Andersen

The Night Before Christmas
By Clement C. Moore

The Nutcracker
The Story Based on the Ballet